EGMONT
We bring stories to life

First published in Great Britain in 2015 by Egmont UK Limited, 1 Nicholas Road, London, W11 4AN

Written by Catherine Such. Designed by Jeannette O'Toole.

ISBN 978 1 4052 7796 9
60299/1
Printed in Italy

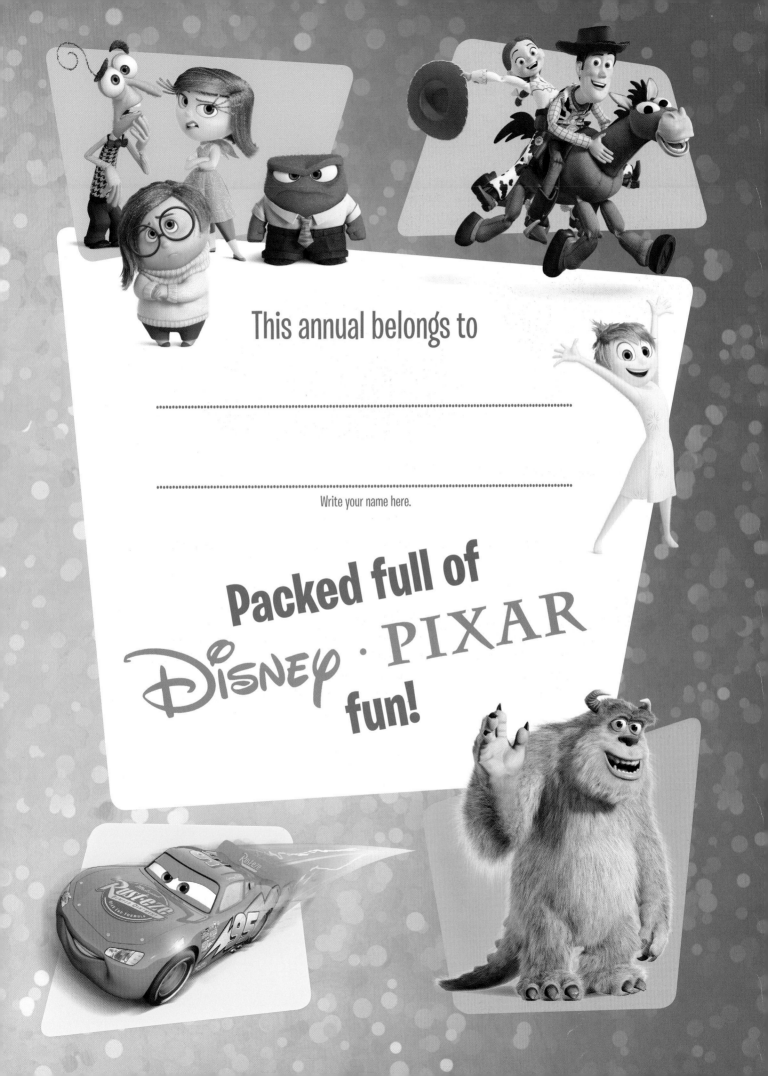

This annual belongs to

....

....

Write your name here.

Packed full of

DISNEY · PIXAR
fun!

Contents

DISNEY · PIXAR

TOY STORY

DISNEY · PIXAR

INSIDE OUT

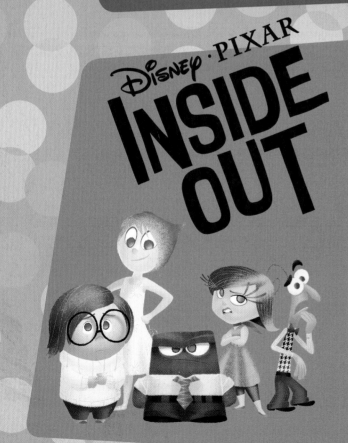

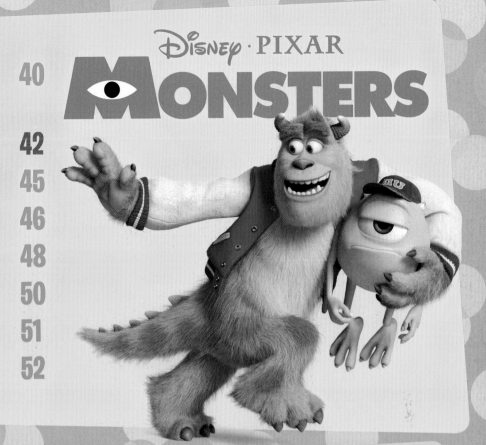

DISNEY · PIXAR

MONSTERS

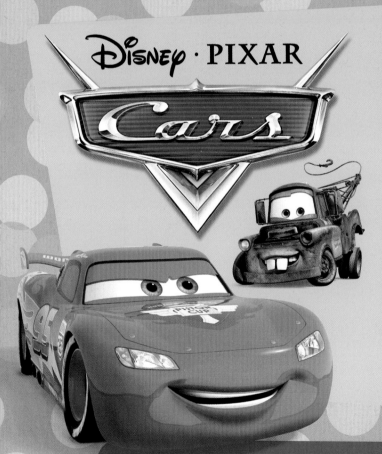

DISNEY · PIXAR

Cars

Disney · PIXAR

TOY STORY

Meet the Gang!
It's playtime! Read on to find out more about your favourite toys.

Woody
Caring cowboy Woody is the leader of the toys. With his trusty horse Bullseye by his side, he'll do anything to make sure the toys stay together.

Buzz Lightyear
Space ranger Buzz is brave and fearless. He looks out for his friends and protects them from danger.

Jessie

Yodelling cowgirl Jessie is full of fun. There's never a dull moment with her around. Yee-ha!

Rex

Rex may look scary but he's the kindest dinosaur in the playroom. His heart is much bigger than his roar.

Mr. Potato Head

Funny Mr. Potato Head makes his friends laugh. He's forever losing his parts or putting them back in the wrong place!

P A L Y

Building Fun

Can you rearrange these blocks to spell a fun word?

_____

Answer on page 67.

Puzzle Mania

The Toy Story gang need your help to finish these fun activities.

Shadow Match

Colour the star next to the shadow that belongs to Buzz.

A

B

C

D

The Wrong Woody

Which Woody is the odd one out?

A ☐

B ☐

C ☐

D ☐

Alien Invasion!

How many Aliens can you count? Write your answer in the circle.

Answers on page 67.

Toys that Time Forgot

Bonnie is excited, she's going to her friend Mason's for a playdate. "This will be fun," she tells Trixie, Woody, Buzz and Rex, as she packs them into her backpack.

But when they arrive at Mason's house, he's playing a new computer game. "There's no way we're gonna get played with today!" wails Rex, as Bonnie throws her backpack full of toys on the floor and goes to play the computer game instead.

The toys creep out of the bag and Trixie notices a box lying on the floor. "Battlesaurus: The Ultimate Dinosaurs," reads Trixie. "Mason's got a new toy."

Suddenly, the friends are surrounded by fierce-looking toys they've never seen before. "This will be the best playtime ever!" Trixie squeals. But the friends don't realise that the new toys aren't playing - they don't even know they're toys!

"I am Reptillious Maximus," says one of the toys, looking at Trixie and Rex. "These fearsome dinosaurs can stay to do battle." Trixie and Rex are so excited, they don't notice Woody and Buzz being silently captured by the other Battlesaurs!

Soon Trixie and Rex are standing in the Arena of Woe, dressed for battle. "I bet you have the most amazing playtimes," sighs Trixie. "Play. Times," Reptillious replies, confused. "I ... do not understand." Trixie laughs, Reptillious seems to be taking the game very seriously!

Just then, a loud cry fills the playroom, "Time for battle!". Trixie and Rex eagerly bound onto the stage. Suddenly, Woody and Buzz are shoved up too. Trixie is shocked as Reptillious lunges at her friends. She thought they were just going to pretend, like they do with Bonnie! "The Battlesaurs are not playing!" warns Woody. "They don't even know they're toys!"

Trixie realises she needs Bonnie's help to save Woody and Buzz. She rushes towards the room where Bonnie and Mason are playing the computer game with Reptillious following her. They pass the Battlesaurus box along the way. "See, you're not a Battlesaur," Trixie shouts. "You're a toy." At last, Reptillious understands.

When Trixie reaches the computer room, she pulls the plug and shuts down the game. Mason is just about to turn the computer back on again when Bonnie spots Reptillious. "Ooh, let's play with your new toy instead," she says.

Bonnie and Mason rush around the playroom gathering the rest of their toys. Then they pretend everyone is having a dance party. Reptillious loves it! He's finally discovered how much fun he can have just being a toy.

THE END

Roaring Fun

See how quickly you can solve these fun dinosaur puzzles. **ROAR!**

Can you find Rex's tail?

Pictures

Which picture is **NOT** from the scene?

1

2

3

4

5

Dinosaur Sizes

Can you put these pictures of these dinosaurs in order of size, starting with the shortest?

1

2

3

4

Footprints

Which dinosaur footprint is the odd one out?

1 **2** **3** **4**

Leaves

Trace over the leaves and colour them in so the dinosaurs can find their food.

Answers on page 67.

Slinky Snaps

The toys have taken photos of Slinky dancing to Mike the Tape Recorder.

Which two of these Slinky snaps are exactly the same?

1

2

3

4

Answer on page 67.

Rope Trails

Sheriff Woody is practising his lassoing skills.

Put on your sheriff's belt and badge and have some cowboy fun! **Yee-haa!**

Who has Woody caught with his lasso? Follow the trails to find out.

START

Alien

Jessie

Slinky

Answer on page 67.

Fun and Games

It's playtime at Sunnyside Daycare! Join in the fun by answering these questions.

Giddy Up!
Who is riding Bullseye?
Write your answer below.

....

Spot it
Can you spot the ball?

Buzz

Rex

Bullseye

Stretch

Chunk

Colour Fun

Colour in a toy brick every time you spot one in the scene.

Big Baby

Woody

Jessie

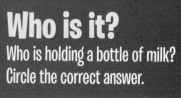

Who is it?

Who is holding a bottle of milk? Circle the correct answer.

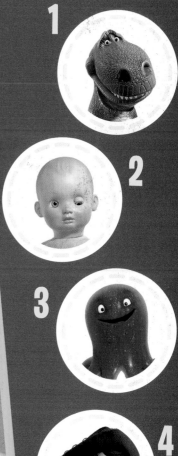

1

2

3

4

Answers on page 67.

Round 'Em Up!

Woody is on a mission to round up these toys. Can you help him by completing each wanted poster?

Add some colour to these wanted posters so the villains won't get away!

WANTED!

Colour Evil Dr. Porkchop!

WANTED!

Use the colour guide below to finish the poster before Lotso gets away!

How many Aliens can you spot on the page?

WANTED!
SUPER VILLAIN

Draw your own super villain here.

WANTED!

Join the dots then colour in Stretch.

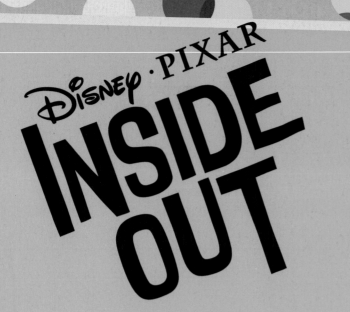

DISNEY · PIXAR INSIDE OUT

Let's meet Riley and go inside her head to find out more about the Emotions that live there ...

Riley

Eleven-year-old Riley is kind and caring. She's a happy girl ... until her family moves to a new city and everything changes.

Joy

Joy is always in a good mood. She loves laughing, chocolate cake and spinning round until she gets dizzy. Joy works hard to keep Riley happy.

Find the Fun!

Sadness

Poor Sadness can't help seeing the downside of things. She'd like to be more positive but finds it so difficult when things go wrong.

A blue sort of day.

Fear

From roller skates and puppies to rain and strange noises, Fear sees danger in everything. His job is to protect Riley and keep her safe.

Ahhhh!

Disgust

Disgust is very proud of her refined tastes. Her job is to keep Riley away from horrible things, such as broccoli and boys!

Ewwww!

Anger

Anger makes sure everything is fair in Riley's life. He tries to keep his cool but it's so hard when there's so much to get worked up about!

GrrrRRR!

Colour the heart next to your favourite Emotion.

Inside Mind World

The Emotions
Joy, Sadness, Fear, Anger and Disgust are the five Emotions that live inside Riley's mind. They control her actions and feelings.

Headquarters
The Emotions live and work inside Headquarters, which is located in the centre of Riley's mind. They use a control panel called a console to do their job.

Memories
Every day, the Emotions help create new memories for Riley which are stored on the shelves inside Headquarters or saved in the core memory holder.

Eye Spy
Can you match each pair of eyes to the correct Emotion?

1   2   3   4   5

a   b   c   d   e

Answers on page 67.

Adventure in Mind World

Read the story and when you see a picture, shout out the correct name.

Joy

Sadness

Anger

Fear

Disgust

Inside Riley's mind lived , , , and - the five Emotions that controlled her actions and feelings.

The Emotions each had a special job to do. kept Riley happy, made sure Riley got help when she needed it, made sure everything was fair, kept Riley safe and protected her from horrible things.

They worked inside Headquarters, the control centre in the middle of Riley's mind. The Emotions took it in turns to use the console that helped them do their job.

If Riley was feeling unhappy, would take over the console and use the levers and buttons to change Riley's actions and make her feel happy again.

Everything was just fine until Riley and her family moved away. Until then, had made sure that the Emotions only created happy memories for Riley, but in her new school, far away from her friends, Riley felt sad.

One day, a new sad memory was created. As tried to stop it being stored forever in Riley's long term memory, she and were accidentally sucked out of Headquarters into Mind World! All of Riley's happy memories were sucked out with them.

(Joy) was worried that Riley wouldn't be happy without her. She didn't want to leave (Fear), (Anger), and (Disgust) in control of the console.

(Joy) and (Sadness) didn't know their way around Mind World but they knew they had to get back to Headquarters with Riley's happy memories as quickly as they could.

On their journey, (Joy) and (Sadness) visited the far reaches of Riley's mind. They met Bing Bong, Riley's imaginary childhood friend, visited French Fry Forest and rode the Train of Thought that delivered daydreams to be stored.

Eventually and made it back to Headquarters with Riley's happy memories.  was very pleased to see them as an unhappy Riley was just about to run away, back to her old town and old friends.

 took control of the console and managed to change Riley's mind. Instead of running away, Riley went back home to her mum and dad and told them how unhappy she'd been feeling. Talking it through made Riley feel better.

A little while later, everything was back on track. Riley had settled into her new home, liked her new school and had made new friends.  had done a great job making their girl happy again.

THE END

Tricky Teasers

The Emotions need your help. See how quickly you can solve these fun Inside Out puzzles.

Missing Piece

The Emotions are hard at work inside Riley's mind. Which jigsaw piece completes the picture?

1

2

3

30

Mad Match

Anger is getting madder and madder! Can you draw lines to match these pictures into pairs? Which picture isn't part of a pair?

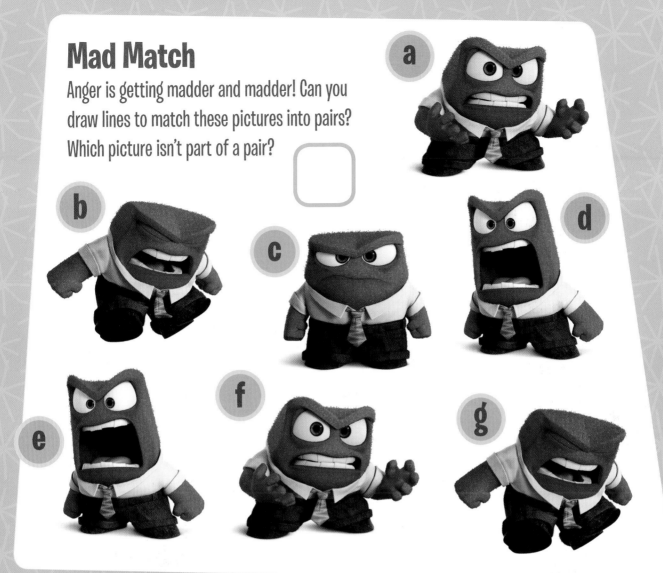

Sadness Sizes

Can you put these pictures of Sadness in order of size, starting with the smallest?

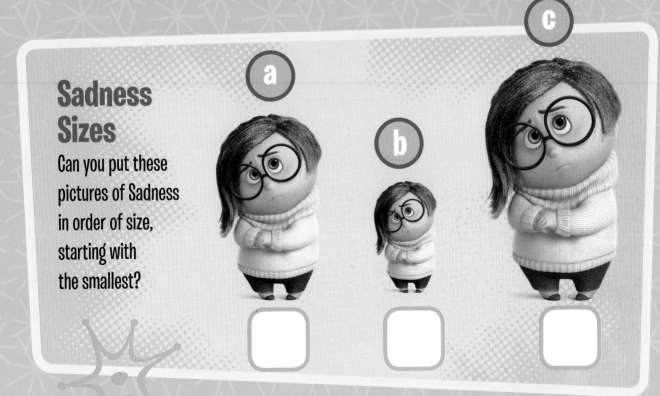

Teamwork

The Emotions work together to keep Riley happy. Add some bright colours to this picture of the team.

Memory Maze

Can you guide Joy through the maze from start to finish? Make sure you collect all Riley's happy memories.

START

FINISH

Answer on page 67.

Odd One Out

Look carefully at these pictures of Joy, Fear and Disgust. Can you spot the odd one out in each row?

1 a b c d

2 a b c d

3 a b c d

Puzzle Fun

Join the Emotions inside Headquarters to complete these awesome activities.

Close-up Clues

Draw lines to match these close-ups to the correct Emotion.

1

2

3

4

5

Fear   Anger   Sadness   Disgust   Joy

Find the Names

Can you find the names of the five Emotions hidden in this wordsearch? Tick a box as you spot each one.

S	A	D	N	E	S	S
D	H	I	Q	S	L	O
V	A	S	K	F	E	A
Z	F	G	A	W	I	N
J	M	U	G	H	S	G
O	A	S	I	L	F	E
Y	A	T	F	E	A	R

☑ JOY

☑ SADNESS

☑ FEAR

☑ ANGER

☑ DISGUST

Colour Code

Copy the letters below into their matching coloured circles to discover Joy's favourite thing to do.

○ ○ ○ ○ ○

H A U L G

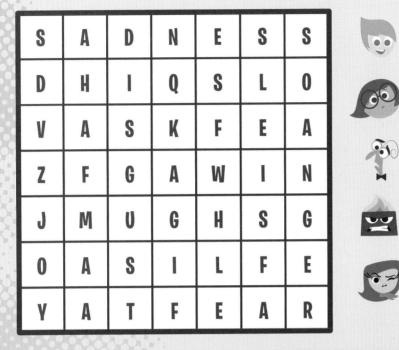

Answers on page 67.

Shadow Shapes

Draw lines to match each Emotion to their correct shadow.

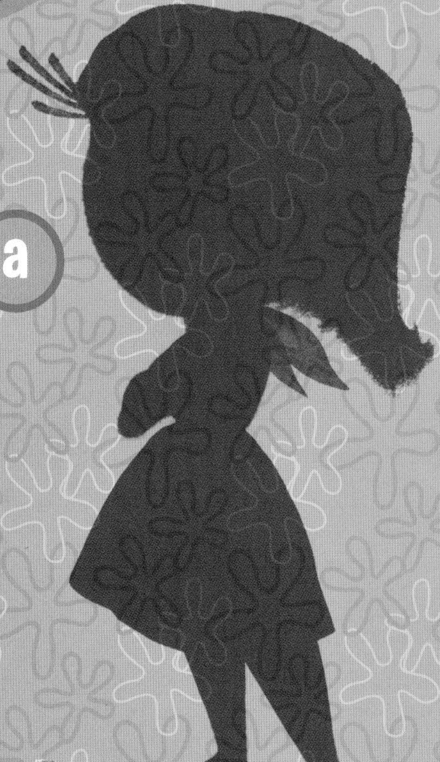

a

b

1

2

38

3

4

5

c

d

Whose shadow is missing?

MONSTERS

Meet the Monsters ...

Mike

Misfit Mike is confident and hardworking. He may not be the scariest monster in class but he's determined to succeed.

Randy

Shy Randy has the amazing ability to change colour so he can blend into any background. He'll do anything to impress his confident classmates.

Sulley

Natural scarer Sulley is loud, funny and full of life. With awesome strength and a fierce roar, he's the big monster around campus.

Johnny

The leader of the Roar Omega Roar fraternity, super-confident Johnny is the top scaring student at MU.

Dean Hardscrabble

As head of the Scaring Program, Dean Hardscrabble terrifies her students. This tough teacher is hard to impress but always gets results.

R	O	A	R	O	R
O	R	O	A	R	O
A	O	A	R	O	A
R	A	R	O	A	R
O	R	O	A	R	O
A	O	R	O	A	R

Scary Search

How many times can you find the word **ROAR** hidden horizontally or vertically in this wordsearch?

Answers on page 68.

Mike's Training

1 Mike had enrolled at Monsters University and was taking a tour of the campus. He picked up a leaflet about the Scare Games. "The Scare Games! A super-intense scaring competition," a monster told him. "You get a chance to prove you're the best." Mike knew he had to enter.

2 After Mike and his rival Sulley were kicked off the Scaring Program, Mike joined the OKs to compete for the Scare Games. But ...

3 ... the team needed one more member - Sulley! Mike knew they couldn't do it without him. It was their last chance to get back on the Scaring Program.

Boo!

Which one of these Scare Games posters is the odd one out?

a

b

c

d

Answer on page 68.

4 After the first disastrous challenge, Mike asked the OKs to show him their special talents. Mike realised they had a lot of work to do.

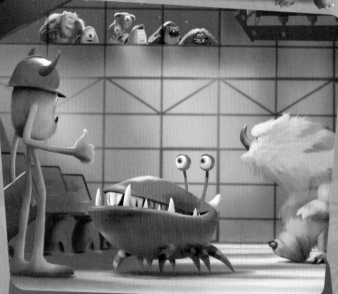

5 Mike secretly took the OKs to the Monsters, Inc. factory to watch the Scare Floor. "The best Scarers use their differences to their advantage," said Mike.

6 The OKs were inspired by what they had seen at Monsters, Inc. Maybe they could do well in the Scare Games after all! Mike began a tough training programme.

7 He taught the team how to avoid parents and teenagers, how to hide and how to be quick on their feet. The OKs worked as a team and Mike and Sulley finally became great friends.

8 All of Mike's training and a strong team spirit paid off. The OKs made it through to the final of the Scare Games. Nobody could believe that they had come so far! Mike was very proud of his misfit monster teammates. No matter what the outcome of the final was, being different and working hard together had made them a super strong team.

THE END

About the story

1 What was the name of Mike's University?

2 What competition did Mike want to enter?

3 Who was Mike's rival before becoming his friend?

4 Did Mike's team make it to the final of the Scare Games?

5 What made the OKs a super-strong team?

Answers on page 68.

Campus Colouring

Mike and Sulley are ready for a new term at Monsters University. Add some bright colours to this fun picture.

It's Scare Time!

The OKs have made it to the final of the Scare Games and they are celebrating!

Differences

There are six scary differences between these two pictures. Colour in an OK flag every time you spot one.

Teamwork!

The RORs can't figure out how the Oozma Kappas managed to come so far. Tick the ROR team members.

1

2

3

4

5 ☐

6 ☑

We Won!
Trace over the Scare Games trophy then colour it in.

Monster Maze

Help Sulley and Mike take the right path to Dean Hardscrabble's Scaring class.

Collect everything they need along the way, ticking them off at the bottom of the page.

START

48

FINISH

Answer on page 68.

Mike's Homework

Mike is doing his Monsters University homework.

Use the monster code to find out which subject Mike is studying.

C E G M Y R N A S

Now colour this monster badge.

Answer on page 68.

50

Training Time

Mike is meeting the OKs for training.

Which of these three paths should Mike take to reach them?

JOX
Jaws Theta Chi

OKs
Oozma Kappa

RORs
Roar Omega Roar

a

b

c

Answer on page 68.

Go Team!

Mike and the OKs are training hard for the Scare Games. Join in Mike's training session by solving these activities.

Grab the Flag

The OKs are training for Avoid the Parent. Tick the matching OK flag so Squishy knows which to take.

a   b   c   d

ROAR!   ROAR!   ROAR!

ROAR!

ROAR!

ROAR!

Great Coach

Mike is coaching the OKs to improve their roars. How many roars have they done?

Hide and Seek

Every good monster knows how to hide. Colour the picture,
matching the dots, to reveal who is hiding.

Answers on page 68.

53

DISNEY · PIXAR

Cars

Mater

Rusty Mater is an easy-going tow truck. He's Lightning's best friend from Radiator Springs.

Vrooming Vehicles!

From secret weapons to rusty hooks, these cars have it all! Let's find out more ...

Lightning

Super speedy Lightning McQueen is a red racing car who dreams of winning the World Grand Prix.

Francesco

Italian racer Francesco is a bit of a show off. This super speedster is his own biggest fan!

Finn

Finn McMissile is a brave Secret Agent. Cool and calm under pressure, he always catches the bad guys.

Holley

Young Secret Agent Holley Shiftwell is a sleek sports car. She's fully equipped with the latest high-tech gadgets.

Tyre Tracks

Lightning has been zooming around. Follow the trail he's left with your finger or a pencil.

Let's Race

Lightning and Francesco are head-to-head on the starting grid ready for the race!

Study these extreme close-ups as quickly as possible. Which close-ups don't belong in this picture?

1

2

3

4

Answers on page 68.

Podium Places

The competition is over. Where did these cars finish?

There's an empty place on the podium for each race. Which of the three champs is missing? Write the letter in the boxes.

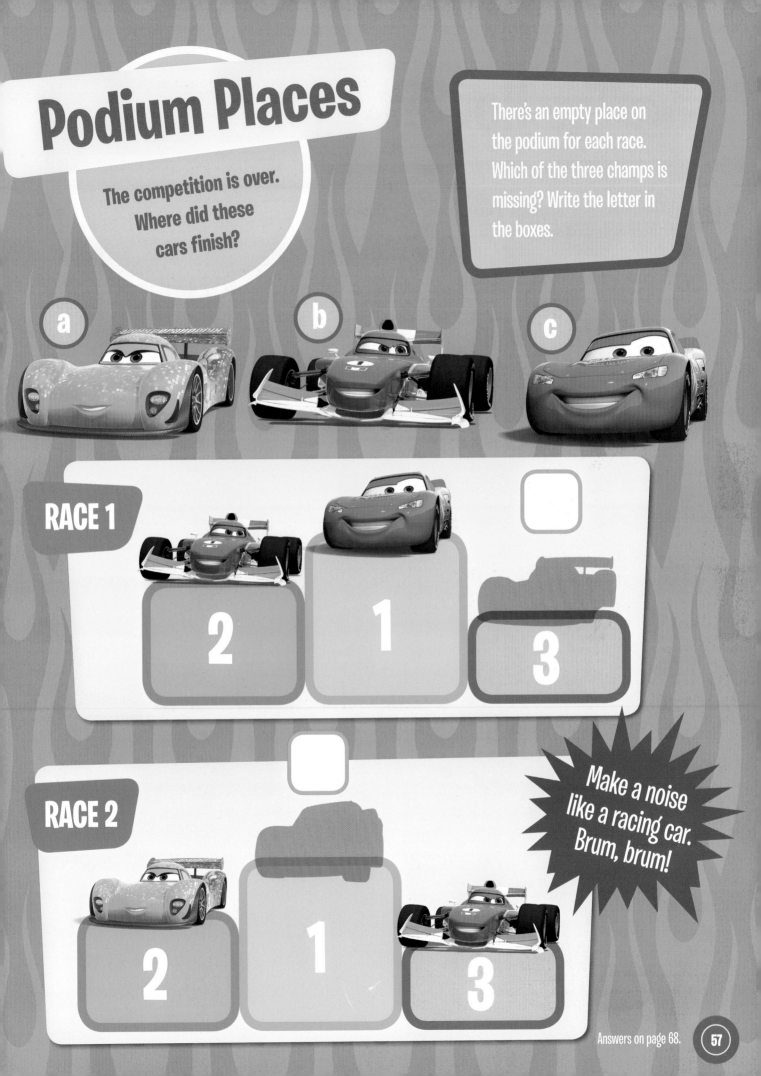

a

b

c

RACE 1

2

1

3

RACE 2

1

2

3

Make a noise like a racing car. Brum, brum!

Answers on page 68.

Hometown Heroes

1 Lightning McQueen and his pit crew arrived in Porto Corsa, Italy, for the World Grand Prix. Luigi and Guido were thrilled to be in their hometown again! "Luigi! Guido!" cried Uncle Topolino. "Welcome home, boys!" All of their friends and family welcomed Luigi and Guido home.

2 Luigi and Guido were proud to introduce their friend, Lightning McQueen, to everyone. He was a real Grand Prix race car!

3 The crowd admired Lightning's sleek body. "Mr McQueen, how you going to beat Francesco Bernoulli in tomorrow's race?" asked Uncle Topolino.

Which is the smallest tyre?

a  b c d e f

Answer on page 68.

4 "Simple! I just have to make sure he's always behind me!" said Lightning. "What a funny American Luigi bring home," laughed Uncle Topolino.

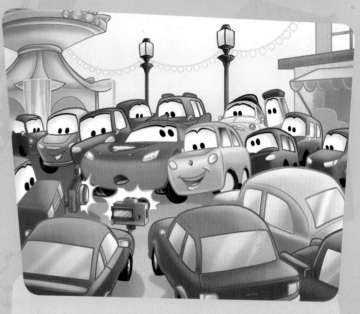

5 Everyone in Porto Corsa wanted to talk to a real American race car. But Lightning could see his friends Luigi and Guido felt left out.

6 "All our friends and family, they only want to talk to a real race car, eh Guido?" said Luigi, sadly. "They forget about Luigi and Guido!" "Si!" said Guido.

7 Lightning saw his friends drive away and told the crowd, "I may drive fast but I couldn't win without Luigi and Guido!"

8 "Come on, guys," said Lightning. "Show your hometown what you can do!" Luigi and Guido set to work, changing Lightning's tyres in just four seconds!

9 The crowd were amazed. "Four tyres in four seconds!" said Uncle Topolino. "Guido and Luigi are fantastico!" "Yep!" said Lightning. "They're the best!"

THE END

About the story

1. Why are Lightning and his friends in Italy?

2. Why are Luigi and Guido so happy to be in Porto Corsa?

3. Why does everyone love Lightning so much?

4. Why do Luigi and Guido feel left out?

5. Who can change 4 tyres in 4 seconds?

Answers on page 68.

Super Speeder!

Lightning is ready to race. Help him on his way by adding some fast colours to this picture.

Ready, Steady, Go!

The racers are lining up for the start of a World Grand Prix race.

Tick each racer when you spot them on the starting line.

Let's Go!
How many cars are in the race? **6** or **7**

Colour in the starting flag so the cars can begin their race.

Who's Missing?
Scribble over the car that is **NOT** in the race.

a

b

Letters
Where is the race? Rearrange these letters to find out.

TkoOy

Answers on page 68.

New Paint Job

Ramone has just given these cars a new paint job. Can you match each car to the paints he used?

1

2

3

86

htB

4

43

5

a

b

c

d

e

Answers on page 68.

Circuit Practice

The racers are practising before the competition begins.

The cars are driving really quickly. Can you work out which blurred pictures are of Lightning McQueen?

1

2

3

4

5

6

Add some snappy colours to the camera cars.

Answers on page 68.

Starting Grid

How to Play

The Cars are on the starting grid. Play this fun game with a friend.

Take it in turns to draw a line from one point of the grid to another along the white lines. Add a point to your scoreboard if you complete a square. The player with the most points after all of the squares have been completed wins!

Player 1 ○○○○○ ○○○○○

Player 2 ○○○○○ ○○○○○

Answers

Missing Piece: 2.
Mad Match: a and f, b and g, d and e.
c isn't part of a pair.
Sadness Sizes: b, a, c.

Pages 8-9 **Meet the Gang**
Building Fun: Play.

Pages 10-11 **Puzzle Mania**
Shadow Match: C.
The Wrong Woody: C.
Alien Invasion!: 10.

Pages 16-17 **Roaring Fun**
Rex's tail is to the right of Rex.
Pictures: 1.
Dinosaur Sizes: 3, 2, 1 and 4.
Footprints: 2.

Page 18 **Slinky Snaps**
2 and 3 are the same.

Page 19 **Rope Trails**
Woody has caught Jessie.

Pages 20-21 **Fun and Games**
Giddy Up!: Buzz.
Spot it: The ball is underneath Woody's foot.
Who is it?: 2 - Big Baby.

Pages 22-23 **Round 'Em Up!**
There are three aliens.

Pages 24-25 **Inside Out**
Eye Spy: 1 - b, 2 - e, 3 - d, 4 - a, 5 - c.

Page 34 **Memory Maze**

Page 35 **Odd One Out**
1. d.   **2.** b.   **3.** c.

Pages 36-37 **Puzzle Fun**
Close-up Clues:
1 - Sadness, 2 - Disgust, 3 - Anger, 4 - Fear, 5 - Joy.
Find the Names:

S	A	D	N	E	S	S
D	H	I	Q	S	L	O
V	A	S	K	F	E	A
Z	F	G	A	W	I	N
J	M	U	G	H	S	G
O	A	S	I	L	F	E
Y	A	T	F	E	A	R

Colour Code: Laugh.

Pages 38-39 **Shadow Shapes**
1 - d, 3 - b, 4 - a, 5 - c.
Sadness's shadow (number 2) is missing.

Answers

Pages 40-41 Meet the Monsters
Scary Search: 9 times.

R	O	A	R	O	R
O	R	O	A	R	O
A	O	A	R	O	A
R	A	R	O	A	R
O	R	O	A	R	O
A	O	R	O	A	R

Pages 42 Mike's Training
Boo!: b.
1. Monsters University.
2. The Scare Games.
3. Sulley.
4. Yes.
5. Being different and working together.

Pages 46-47 It's Scare Time!

Teamwork: 1, 3 and 6.

Pages 48-49
Monster Maze

Page 50 Mike's Homework
Mike is studying Scream Energy.

Page 51 Training Time
Mike should take path b.

Pages 52-53 Go Team!
Grab the Flag: b.
Great Coach: 6 roars.

Page 56 Let's Race
1 and 4.

Page 57 Podium Places
Race 1 - a, Race 2 - c.

Pages 58-60 Hometown Heroes
d is the smallest tyre.
1. For the World Grand Prix.
2. It's their hometown.
3. He's a real race car.
4. Everyone wants to talk to Lightning.
4. Luigi and Guido.

Pages 62-63 Ready, Steady, Go!
Let's Go!: 6.
Who's Missing?: b.
Letters: TOKYO.

Page 64 New Paint Job
1 - b, 2 - c, 3 - d, 4 -a, 5 - e.

Page 65 Circuit Practise
1 and 6.